DISASTER DIARIES

ZOMBIES!

DISASTER DIARIES

Zombies!

Aliens!

Brainwashed!

DISASTER DIARIES

ZOMBIES!

R. McGEDDON
ILLUSTRATED BY JAMIE LITTLER

[Imprint]
MAKE YOUR MARK

NEW YORK

Special thanks to Barry Hutchison

[Imprint]
MAKE YOUR MARK

A part of Macmillan Children's Publishing Group

DISASTER DIARIES: ZOMBIES! Text copyright © 2014 by Hothouse Fiction
Ltd. Illustrations copyright © 2014 by Jamie Littler. All rights reserved.
Printed in the United States of America by R. R. Donnelley & Sons
Company, Harrisonburg, Virginia. For information, address Imprint,
175 Fifth Avenue, New York, N.Y. 10010.

Beware the curse upon this book
If from the rightful owner took:
A plague of undead ghouls unleashed
On thieving little fingers feast!

Library of Congress Cataloging-in-Publication Data is available.
ISBN 978-1-250-09084-3 (hardcover) / ISBN 978-1-250-09085-0 (ebook)

Our books may be purchased in bulk for promotional, educational,
or business use. Please contact your local bookseller or the Macmillan
Corporate and Premium Sales Department at (800) 221-7945 ext. 5442 or
by e-mail at MacmillanSpecialMarkets@macmillan.com.

Imprint logo designed by Amanda Spielman

First published in Great Britain in 2014 by Little, Brown Books for
Young Readers

First U.S. Edition—2016

10 9 8 7 6 5 4 3 2 1

mackids.com

FOR GEORGE A. ROMERO,
KING OF THE LIVING DEAD

CHAPTER ONE

Professor Pamplemousse was a small man by anyone's standards. Many of the boys in his class, and some of the girls, too, towered several inches above him. This made him nervous, but so did goldfish, corrugated cardboard, and certain colors of paint, so that wasn't saying much.

Sometimes, though, even the shortest men can have a commanding presence about them, earning respect from everyone they meet without having to say a word. This *could* be said about Professor Pamplemousse, but it would be a lie. The professor didn't have a commanding presence; he barely

1

had a presence at all. In fact, he'd often lie awake at night wondering if he even existed. Unfortunately for him, he did.

"Right, s-settle down, everyone," he called, trying to quiet the rowdy classroom. "Hello? Can anyone actually hear me?"

Maybe the students in Pamplemousse's science class could hear him. Maybe they couldn't. If they could, they didn't let on. Instead, they laughed and chatted and watched the clock as it ticked its way toward the final few minutes of the final day of the final week of the school term. It was almost vacation time, and whatever the professor was up to with Bunsen burners and petri dishes and all that stuff, no one was giving two hoots.

Near the back of the class, Sam Saunders and his best friend, Arty Dorkins, were planning their summer antics. Sam was one of those

kids in school who was liked by everyone.
Teachers always gave him slightly higher
grades than they should. His classmates would
offer to carry his bag, and would hardly ever
then throw it into the bushes and run away
laughing. All the lunch ladies fawned over him,
which was one of the reasons why he avoided
the school cafeteria at all costs.

Arty, on the other hand, was not

particularly popular. He wasn't athletic like Sam or charming like Sam, and on the good-looking front he was about a three, which was slightly below the average family dog. Despite their differences, the boys were the best of friends, which just goes to show, doesn't it?

Like most days, the out-of-school activities they were planning involved playing pranks on Arty's older brother, Jesse. They enjoyed doing this for two reasons. First, Arty's older brother wasn't very nice, and second, Arty's older brother wasn't very nice. Technically, this is just one reason, but it's such a good one it's worth saying twice. And now that it was summer vacation and Sam was staying at Arty's for the weekend, they could really go all out.

"What about a trip wire or something?"

Arty suggested. He was bouncing excitedly in his seat, which made his plump torso wobble like a bowl of rice pudding. "We could trip him up and, if we calculate the trajectory correctly, make him fall right on his big, stupid face."

Sam nodded slowly. "Not bad, not bad. It's got potential."

Arty frowned. "There's a 'but' coming, isn't there?"

Sam wrinkled his nose. "Bit obvious, isn't it? I mean, we tripped him up yesterday, didn't we? After he put that liquid soap in your cola."

"We did," said Arty, frowning as he remembered the slimy bubbles frothing out of his nose. "And he fell right on his face."

"Exactly. And while that was brilliant, I think we need to try something more ambitious. Remember that time we dug the ditch to get revenge on Jesse for filling the contents of your lunch box with sand?"

Arty did remember the ditch, and before that, the crunching sensation of biting into a very sandy sandwich. It had taken them a week of planning and fourteen solid hours of digging to pull off the prank, but the sight of Jesse falling into the hole and landing *right on his big, stupid face* had made it all worthwhile.

"Okay . . . okay . . . How about this?" began Arty. His eyes darted left and right, and Sam could almost hear his friend's big brain at work. "What about if we set up some kind of rudimentary lasso snare . . ."

Sam's chair creaked as he leaned forward. "Go on."

"We attach it to a tree and tie something to it

that he won't be able to resist. Something that'll lure him in."

"A mirror? He'd love that."

"Right! So he grabs the bait, and the lasso wraps around him and flicks him up into the tree."

"Brilliant!" Sam grinned.

"Then we feed him to a shark."

Sam blinked. "Er . . . what?"

"We feed him to a shark. You know? A great white or something. Some of them have up to three hundred and fifty teeth. Imagine that. It could devour him in seconds."

"Right," said Sam. (Arty had a history of odd suggestions.) He cleared his throat. "Interesting. We *could* go with that plan. . . . Or we could just hide in the bushes and chuck water balloons at him?"

Arty shrugged. "Or we could do that.

Whatever's easiest."

"The water balloons, probably," said Sam.

"Let's do that, then," Arty said, but he made a mental note of the shark idea for future reference.

How to Annoy Your Older Brother

One effective way to make your older brother seethe with rage (without resorting to shark attacks) is by spoiling his much-needed beauty sleep. You could stay awake all night to do this, but that sounds a bit tiring to me. Here's another method.

You will need:

- 1 brother

- 1 alarm clock

- A basic grasp of telling time

Sneak into your brother's bedroom when he's not there.

Set the alarm for a random time during the night. Possible random times include 3:14 AM, 2:46 AM, and 4:03 AM.

Hide the alarm clock in an annoying place, like the top shelf of his closet.

Go to bed at your usual time.

Laugh yourself to sleep.

At the front of the class, Professor Pamplemousse was pouring something boring into something dull. "Look, trust me, you're going to like this," he said. "It's green, yes? Now behold as before your very eyes it turns a *very slightly* different shade of green."

The professor stared into his test tube,

watching the mixture bubble and froth. "Oh, it's gone purple," he muttered. "Why has it gone purple? It's not supposed to go—"

A paper airplane performed an emergency crash landing on the back of Pamplemousse's head, its nose cone tangling in his wispy white locks. He spun on the spot, the test tube still clutched in his hand, the origami jet still protruding from his hair.

"Children, please," he said, trying to appeal to their better nature. "I know we're all excited, but throwing paper airplanes in a science lab is dangerous. It could've taken someone's eye out. Luckily, I was here to make sure you were all unhurt. No, please, don't thank me. Your safety is my number one concern."

He had been hoping for some sort of reaction to that last part. A grateful cheer, perhaps, for his selfless heroism. Yet nobody paid him the slightest bit of attention, so he said it again, louder this time.

"I was saying . . . don't thank me. Your safety is my number one—"

Right then, the test tube in his hand exploded, spraying fizzing purple goo over Simon Stumble, a boy in the front row. This was just Simon's luck. Bad things always happened when Simon Stumble was around, and they tended to happen to Simon himself. He was growing too fast, the school nurse said. His brain couldn't keep up with his lanky limbs and awkwardly huge feet. He was accident-prone with a capital "AAAAAAARGH!"

In the past month alone, Simon had broken three toes, lost a nostril, and accidentally declared war on the Netherlands. So while

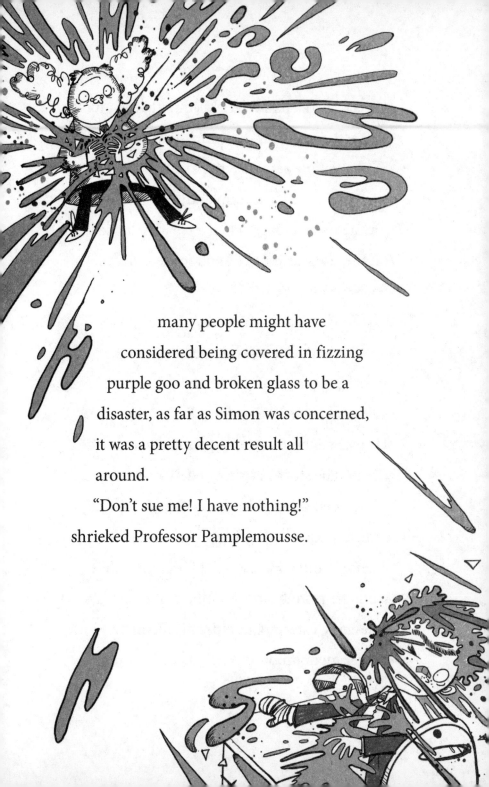

many people might have
considered being covered in fizzing
purple goo and broken glass to be a
disaster, as far as Simon was concerned,
it was a pretty decent result all
around.

"Don't sue me! I have nothing!"
shrieked Professor Pamplemousse.

He clamped a hand over his mouth, then took a steadying breath. "By which I mean: Here, Simon, let me get you a tissue."

A few rows back, Sam and Arty reached for their schoolbags. Their eyes were locked on the clock as it ticked and tocked the final few seconds away.

"Ten," cried Sam. "Nine!"

The rest of the class joined in. "Eight, seven."

Sam glanced sideways at Simon Stumble. He was dabbing at the purple goo with a tissue. The stuff was smeared all over his face, from forehead to chin. It didn't look healthy— in fact, it looked positively, noxiously, toe-curlingly infectious. Some of it dangled like a booger from his nose. Some of it fizzed like a dancing caterpillar across his distinctive ginger monobrow.

"Six, five, three," cried the students, who never paid any attention in math, either. "Two, one!"

Brrrrrrrriiiiiiiiiiiing!

Twenty-five sets of chair legs scraped across the floor as twenty-five students leaped to their feet. School was over. Summer had begun. As they rushed for the door, many of the students agreed that life was good and that nothing could possibly go wrong.

Silly, silly students.

"I hope Simon's okay," said Sam.

Arty managed a glance back into the classroom. Simon looked back at him, his mouth hanging open. His eyes were wide and bulging, his face was gray, and he slowly lifted his arms out in front of him. Arty felt a shiver travel down his spine. "Erm, yeah," he said. "I'm not so sure about that." But before they could turn back, Sam and Arty were being swept helplessly through the door in a tidal wave of vacation-hungry students.

In a cloud of cheers, schoolbags, and happiness, the boys bustled out through the school gates and into the start of the summer. Poor Simon, however, was left to undergo an un-deadly transformation. . . .

Sam and Arty's Summer To-Do List (as compiled in a constructive final science lesson of the year)

- Become famous.

- Build a rocket.

- Eat Arty's body weight in french fries.

- Discover treasure.

- Chase a robber.

- Grow taller.

- Join the army.

- Leave the army.

- Find a new smell.

- Acquire a shark (Arty only).

CHAPTER TWO

On the first, sunny morning of vacation, Emmie Lane crept down the stairs without stepping on a single one of them. The stairs in her aunt's house were old and creaky, and one squeaky floorboard could be enough to give her away. She slid slowly down the banister instead, in stealth mode, wearing all black and barely making a sound. It was really quite impressive. But then Emmie was really quite an impressive girl when she wanted to be.

Emmie lived with her great-aunt Doris for reasons far too horrible and upsetting to go into. Seriously, I'm welling up just thinking about it. The terrible thing we're not going to speak of happened when Emmie was quite young. When she'd first moved to the town of Sitting Duck, she'd thought it a very strange place, full of odd things and odder people. In the years since then, though, she'd come to love all of its little quirks, and she couldn't think of anywhere else she'd rather call home. . . .

Except New York, Paris, London, Melbourne, and the moon. Apart from those places, Sitting Duck was exactly where she wanted to be.

She could hear Doris down in the kitchen. It sounded like the mad old bat was clanging something with a frying pan. This was very unusual behavior. Mondays and Thursdays were her usual days for clanging things with frying pans, so why she was clanging away on a Saturday was anyone's guess.

Emmie wasn't complaining, though. If Great-Aunt Doris was busy in the kitchen, it would make her escape that much easier. She slid down the final few inches of the rickety old banister and got ready to make the final leap onto the swirly brown carpet at the bottom of the stairs. It wasn't an easy jump to make, but once she'd made it, the front door would be within reach. She was almost free. One final leap—

There was a hiss from around the corner at the bottom of the stairs. A fat black cat with wiry hair padded into view. He sat down slowly and stared up at Emmie as she clung to the banister like a spider.

Emmie froze. This was bad. The cat, Attila, didn't like her. He didn't like anyone,

as far as she could tell, but he disliked her in particular. He could also screech louder than any living creature she'd ever met. If he kicked off now, Doris would come running, frying pans or no frying pans. The cat was directly in her path. There was no way of getting past with him sitting there.

With great difficulty, Emmie managed to

wriggle a hand into her pocket. She pulled out a small fish-shaped treat, which she carried for just such an emergency. "Look. Want it?" she said.

Attila's eyes flicked lazily from Emmie to the treat and back again. Slowly, ever so slowly, the cat shook his head. He wrinkled his little pink nose. Then he opened his mouth and got ready to screech.

Quick as a flash, Emmie flicked the treat into the cat's wide-open gob. The cat hacked and coughed as the fishy treat wedged at the back of his throat. His eyes went wide. His tail stood straight up. With a final splutter, Attila shot off in search of his water bowl, leaving the way clear for Emmie to jump to safety. She pulled open the front door, dashed along the path, and vaulted the garden gate before Attila had drunk his first drop.

Escaping Great-Aunt Doris

Not everyone is unlucky enough to have a Great-Aunt Doris, but it's still a good idea to know the best ways to escape your house, just in case an unexpected great-aunt turns up out of the blue some day and starts being all "kissy, kissy for Auntie."

Every house is different, but some useful ways of escaping might include:

- Climbing down the drainpipe

- Making a ladder out of bedsheets

- Disguising yourself as a lamp, then creeping toward the door an inch at a time

- Turning invisible

But anyway, back to Emmie. Once outside she ducked out of sight behind the fence and took a minute to get her breath back. A pair of expensive designer shoes stepped into view. Not on their own, obviously—they were attached to the feet of Phoebe Bowles.

Phoebe had only lived in Sitting Duck for a few months, but already she'd established herself as the most irritating person Emmie had ever met. She was more or less Emmie's exact opposite. Phoebe enjoyed things like makeovers and pedicures and reality TV shows full of people called Chad, whereas Emmie hated all that stuff. Especially people called Chad.

"OMG," prattled Phoebe, sounding, as always, like she was speaking through her nose. "What are you doing on the ground, Em?"

Emmie looked up. Phoebe's delicate features were pulled into a frown, and a breeze had blown her long blond hair into the shape of a question mark above her head.

"Sitting down," Emmie said.

Phoebe shook her head. "Okay, well, if you want to hang out with me, sitting down is, like, a no-no."

"I don't want to hang out with you." Emmie shrugged, but she stood up anyway.

Phoebe, selective hearing enabled, chose to gloss over what she was sure must have been a joke on Emmie's part. Emmie shoved her hands in her pockets and walked away from her aunt's house. Phoebe teetered along behind her.

"Seriously, you so crack me up!" Phoebe let out a little gasp. "Oh, hey, you know what we should do?"

"Sew our mouths shut?" Emmie suggested.

"Better. We should totally go to the spa!"

Emmie rolled her eyes. *Here we go again*, she thought.

"Sitting Duck doesn't have a spa," she said. "Besides, I'm meeting Sam and Arty."

"What kind of town lets its residents go without pedicures?" Phoebe snorted. "In Silver Spoon . . ."

Emmie rolled her eyes. If she had to listen to another story about the gilded hamlet of Silver Spoon, she couldn't possibly be held responsible for her actions. Luckily, Sam and Arty stepped around the corner right on cue.

"Morning, girls," said Sam as he and Arty crossed the road to join them. Sam and Arty had been best friends with Emmie for years, so they knew her secret rendezvous spots well.

"Thank goodness," said Emmie.

"Did you know this town doesn't even have a spa?" Phoebe moaned. "I mean, like, OMG for totes, right?"

"Right," said Sam, his head bobbing up and down like a nodding dog's.

"Right," agreed Arty, doing the same. He leaned in closer to Sam. "What's she saying?"

"I have no idea," Sam whispered back.

"So," said Emmie, doing her best to ignore Phoebe completely. "What's the plan?"

Sam and Arty exchanged an excited

glance. "We're going to pelt my big brother with water balloons," Arty announced.

Phoebe let out a gasp of horror. "Jesse?"

"Yes," said Arty.

"Water balloons?"

"Yes," said Sam.

Phoebe's face went pale. "OMG, you can't. Not Jesse! The only reason I'm hanging out with you lose—ahem . . . erm . . ." She rested a hand lightly against her forehead. "Somebody catch me. I'm totally going to faint!"

Phoebe swooned dramatically. The other three watched as she fell backward onto the ground. They stood staring at her for ages.

"I think you were meant to catch her," Emmie said to Sam.

"What?" said Sam. "Why me?"

"Well, I wasn't going to do it," Emmie said.

"And I've got a bit of a sore back," Arty added.

They continued to stare down at Phoebe.

"*Hello?*" Phoebe said. "Isn't someone going to help me up?"

Nobody moved.

Arty turned to Emmie. "You hear what happened to Simon Stumble yesterday?"

"Head stuck in a door?" Emmie guessed.

"Nope."

"Legs set on fire?"

"Nope."

"Lost his other nostril?"

"Nope! Sprayed by weird chemicals from Pamplemousse's lab," Arty said.

"Poor Simon," Emmie said.

"Yeah," agreed Arty and Sam. "Poor Simon."

"Never mind 'poor Simon.'" Phoebe shrieked. "What about poor *me*?"

Sam reached out a hand. "Here, let me help you," he said (because he's nice like that). Phoebe took his hand and he began to pull her up.

"Jesse's coming," Arty hissed. Sam released his grip and Phoebe thudded back down onto the pavement.

"Like . . . *ouch!*"

"Where?" Sam asked.

Arty pointed to the end of the street, where his big brother and one of his friends were strolling along as if they owned the place.

"Where's the ammo?" asked Emmie.

Sam opened his schoolbag. He and Arty had stocked up before heading to meet Emmie. Over a dozen fat water balloons wobbled inside the backpack. Emmie and Arty grabbed three each.

Arty hopped excitedly from foot to foot. "Jesse won't know what hit him."

Phoebe sat up sharply. "Did someone say *Jesse?*"

Emmie splattered one of the balloons across Phoebe's head, the water shocking her into silence.

"Right. Places, everyone," Sam urged as he began to climb a tree, while Arty and Emmie looked for hiding places of their own.

Hiding Places from Which to Launch a Sneak Attack

Good:

- Up a tree

- Behind a bush

- Around a corner

LOOK HERE!!

Bad:

- On top of a distant mountain

- Beneath a giant illuminated arrow with "Look Here!!" written on it

- A raised platform, surrounded by elephants, cheerleaders, and a brass band

Sam wriggled onto a high branch and lay down flat. Sitting Duck spread out below him like a rash. From up there, he could see Rickety Tower, the glass church, and the accordion maker's workshop. Over to his left was the newspaper shop, which was built entirely out of recycled newspapers, and the cake shop, which was built entirely out of bricks and other building materials.

Sam sighed at the sight of it all. Sitting Duck was a funny old place, where nothing out of the ordinary ever happened or was ever likely to.

"Aim for the face," Arty instructed. "Hit him right in his *big, stupid face*."

"Ten-four," replied Sam, turning his attention to matters at hand.

"Will do." Emmie nodded.

Arty ducked behind a bush. He could hear

his brother's big, booming voice droning on about some pointless sporting fact. The water balloon wobbled in Arty's pudgy hand. This was going to be utterly brilliant.

Although, he couldn't help but think, feeding him to a shark would've been even better.

CHAPTER THREE

Water balloons rained down like . . . well, like rain, really. But rain encased in thin rubber. With knots at one end. So, you know, not *exactly* like rain.

They wobbled like wobbly things, fell like fally things, then exploded like explodey things. Suddenly finding himself soaked to the skin, Jesse began to shout. Like an angry thing.

"Wharughrugh!" he bellowed, too enraged to form actual words. "Ifurmingahum!"

No one present was able to speak Angry Jesse, but if they had been, they would have understood the first part of his furious garble to mean: "Gadzooks! I appear to have been set about by pranksters. This has made me most unhappy. A violent, almost certainly bloody vengeance shall be mine." They would also have understood the second part to mean: "I hope I don't look like I've wet myself."

Jesse needn't have worried about that. He didn't look like he'd wet himself. Not unless he had the world's biggest bladder and the world's worst aim—he was soaking wet from head to toe. But his ordeal wasn't over yet.

One more rubber-clad raindrop sailed through the air toward him. If this were a film, we'd follow that raindrop in slow motion as it arced across the bright blue sky. We'd see the gleeful expressions frozen on the faces of Sam, Arty, and Emmie, and watch the faces of Jesse and his friend become fixed in masks of dripping wet horror.

If this were a film, there'd be a swelling of dramatic music or the sound of a heart beating to help ramp up the tension: *Boom-boom. Boom-boom. Boom-boom.*

But it isn't a film, and we don't have any of those things. What we do have is a highly detailed and anatomically accurate picture of water exploding in Jesse's big, confused face.

Okay, so we don't have that, either. But that's exactly what happened, so let's all take a moment to imagine it, and then move on.

Done? Good.

Jesse squelched around to look at his friend. He had taken the brunt of the attack, so the other boy wasn't as wet as Jesse was. That wasn't saying much, though. There were fish swimming in the sea who weren't as wet as Jesse was right at that moment.

Jesse's friend was a hulking beast of a teenager who looked like a cross between a caveman and another, much larger caveman. His name is of absolutely no importance to the rest of the story, so let's just call him "The Brute" (although in actual fact his real name is Ian, but deep down he's never really felt like it suited him, and he might change it when he's older).

"OMG, you're *soaking*!" twittered Phoebe. She jumped to her feet and hurried toward Jesse.

Ker-sploosh! Three water balloons splattered against her one after the other.

Emmie's voice floated out from her hiding place. "Thirty points."

The water had blasted off most of Phoebe's lip gloss and turned her blond hair into something that resembled a partially collapsed bird's nest. She stared at Jesse, breathing heavily as the last of the water trickled down her nose and off her chin. Then, as if it would somehow make her look better, she slapped on some more lip gloss and attempted a shaky smile.

Arty, who had been crouching patiently in the shrubbery, popped up and let fly a final water balloon, but Jesse snatched it from the air. He held the balloon at arm's length, then his hand tightened into a fist, and the balloon gave a soft, soggy *pop*.

Arty, frozen in panic, stared at his brother. Then he ducked and tried to pretend he wasn't there. It didn't work. In two big paces, Jesse was over at the bush. He dragged Arty through the prickly branches and hoisted him into the air, which, considering the size of Arty, was no mean feat.

"You soaked me," Jesse growled. He had a real knack for stating the obvious.

"It was an accident!" Arty said.

"What? You *accidentally* filled a load of water balloons, *accidentally* hid behind a bush, then *accidentally* chucked them at me?" Jesse sneered. "You expect me to believe that?"

"You expect me to believe that liquid soap *accidentally* appeared in my cola?" Arty scoffed. "I was burping bubbles for days!"

"Flatten him," growled The Brute, although at the same time he wondered quietly what he might one day change his name to. Bernard, maybe. Or possibly Abigail. Decisions, decisions.

There was a *swoosh* as Sam swung down from the tree. Right before that, he'd carefully zipped the unused balloons up in the backpack, which—without giving too much away—might be worth remembering for later.

"Back off, Ian," warned Sam, who knew The Brute's real name and thought that it actually suited him in a funny sort of way. "Leave him alone."

"Yeah," said Emmie, stepping out from behind something else. (I think it was a mailbox.) "Let him go."

Jesse scowled. "Or what?"

Emmie heard a door being flung open behind her from the direction of the houses. "Or . . ." she began.

"Oi!" screeched Great-Aunt Doris. "What's goin' on? Whatchoo lot up to? Eh?"

". . . her," Emmie concluded.

"Clear off down yer own end, the lot of you," Doris raged. "I'm warnin' you—I know all yer moms." The old woman's eyes fell on

Emmie. Not literally, of course. That would be

hideous. "You!" she hissed.

Emmie turned and
offered her
sweetest smile,
but Great-Aunt
Doris was
having none of
it. She bounded
along the path,
scrawny arms
flailing, wrinkled
face sagging, rolling
pin swooping and
swishing this way and that.

Doris stopped, as she always did, when she

reached the front gate, and pointed her rolling

pin squarely at Emmie.

"You! You're outside! You're not upstairs," yelped Doris, who could have given Jesse a real run for his money in the stating-the-obvious stakes.

"Hee-hee, now you're in for it," sniggered Jesse. He let go of Arty, allowing him to slump to the ground. "I'll let the crazy old lady deal with you. Then I'll kill you all later."

"Something to look forward to," muttered Sam as Doris launched into a full-scale rant.

"Sneakery!" she shrieked. "Sneakery and tippytoes! Whatchoo think you're doing out there with them and not in here with me?"

"I—"

"I been talking to you for the past ten minutes, an' all," Doris raged. "I wondered why you were bein' so quiet. 'That's not like her,' I said. 'That's not like her being all quiet like that,' I said."

"Well—" Emmie began, trying to get a word in.

"But now we knows why, don't we? Oh yes, now we knows why. Sneakery, that's why! Sneakery and—"

To everyone's relief, something round and fast chose exactly that moment to hit Doris squarely in the face. It was the sort of thing you'd see in *Funniest Home Videos 3* or *Getting Hit in the Face by Things 6*. It sent Doris staggering backward into the garden. Her teeth flew out and landed on the grass. Which wouldn't have been as big a deal if they'd been dentures.

The round thing, which was now not nearly as fast, plopped down into her prized begonias. Dazed from the impact, Doris reached down for it, eyes bleary and gums sore from the impact. "Balls!" she cried. "I hates balls!"

The inside of Doris's shed was like an elephant's graveyard for balls. She'd amassed quite a collection over the years. They were all stored in there, neatly stacked and carefully punctured, and this one was heading there, too.

Her fingers found the spherical object just as the tears that had filled her eyes began to clear. She noticed then that there was something different about this ball. It wasn't perfectly round, for one thing. It had a face, for another. Great-Aunt Doris held it higher, and it was immediately obvious to Sam and the others that it wasn't a ball at all.

It was a human head.

As they watched, the head opened its eyes. Its mouth flapped loosely, letting a purple tongue loll out. The eyes shifted and Arty got a horrible feeling they were shifting to look at him. There was something oddly familiar about the head, he thought. It took him a few moments to realize what it was.

It was the monobrow. The ginger monobrow.

Simon Stumble's mouth gnashed hungrily, and a low groan burst from his bloated lips, demanding:

"Braaaaaiiins!"

CHAPTER FOUR

Great-Aunt Doris took a moment to collect her thoughts. Once she had collected them, they went something like this: *Aaaaaaargh! Run away!*

And so she did. Simon Stumble's head thudded down onto the path as Doris let it drop. She scampered back up the steps and slammed the door behind her.

Then silence fell, broken only by the low moaning of the undead Simon and the squeaky *parp* of The Brute unexpectedly soiling himself. The Brute turned to ask Jesse what they should do, but Jesse had already taken a leaf out of Great-Aunt Doris's book and was running back along the street as fast as his legs would carry him.

"Hey, wait for me," The Brute cried, waddling after him.

Sam, Arty, and Emmie exchanged glances as another mouthful of mournful moaning floated out of Simon's severed head. Cautiously, with Sam taking the lead, they tiptoed across to Great-Aunt Doris's gate and peered down at the path.

Simon stared at them from beneath his ginger monobrow. His pupils were gray and glassy-looking. Emmie gave a shudder when she spotted them.

"Wow," she said. "His eyes are really creepy."

"His *eyes* are creepy?!" Arty

spluttered. "It doesn't bother you that he's just a head?"

Sam leaned over the gate. "Simon, mate," he said, raising his voice a little. "You all right?"

"Of course he's not all right!" Arty said. "What sort of question is that?"

Phoebe had been quietly sulking about the water-balloon-to-the-face incident, but her curiosity finally got the better of her. She strolled over to see what all the fuss was about. She followed the gaze of Sam and the others until she spotted Simon's head on the path. His mouth gnashed open and closed, spraying reddish-black droplets on the stone.

"Whoa," she breathed, her eyes wide with horror. "What is up with that hairstyle? Frizzy is not a good look."

"He's just a head!" Arty yelped. "He doesn't need grooming advice!"

Phoebe snorted. "Trust me, he *totally* does."

"Is he going to be okay, do you think?" asked Emmie.

"Well, I doubt he's going to go mountain biking anytime soon," Sam said. He looked over at Arty. "What are you thinking?"

"That I might be sick."

"I meant about what's going on?" Sam said. "Any ideas?"

"Yeah, come on, let's hear it, Mr. Big Brain," said Emmie.

Down on the ground, Simon's eyes widened. "Braaaaaiiins!"

"I'm . . . I'm not sure."

"Any idea where Simon's head came from?" Sam asked.

Phoebe's hand shot up. "Simon's neck?"

Everyone ignored her, especially Emmie, who ignored her twice as hard as the others did. Arty's lips moved in silent calculation as he worked out the head's trajectory without using his fingers or anything. He's dead clever like that. There isn't a number he hasn't heard of. Seriously. Think of a number. Got one? Arty's heard of it. He's *that* good.

"Based on my calculations," Arty began, "and bearing in mind that my brain is in the process of shutting down through sheer terror, I think the head came from somewhere over . . ."

He spun and pointed off in the direction of the flag shop at the end of the road.

". . . there," he said. Then his face went the color of Professor Pamplemousse's hair. (Flip back if you've forgotten.) (Hint: It's white.)

Shambling along the street toward them, barely even pausing to look in the window of the flag shop—which was a shame, because they stocked a really quite excellent range of flags and flag-related merchandise—were a number of hideous-looking figures. The exact number was six, which, incidentally, Arty had *definitely* heard of.

Their arms were reaching out in front of them, their gnarled fingers clawing at the air. They shuffled and staggered, their feet dragging on the pavement in a way that was sure to annoy moms everywhere. Their skin was gray and rotting, their hair coming out in great dirty clumps. And one of them was just a shambling body, confused as to where he'd thrown his own head.

"They're z-z-z-z," Arty shuttered. "Z-z-z-z—"

"Zombies," Sam whispered. "Wow! I don't believe it."

"W-we should go," Arty suggested.

"Much as I hate to agree with Big Brain . . ." Emmie began.

"Braaaaaiiins!" groaned Simon's head.

Arty shot Emmie an imploring look.

"Stop calling me that—you're giving him ideas!"

"Maybe we

should try to help them or something," Sam said.

Phoebe rested a hand on Sam's arm. "There's nothing we can do for them. It's too late," she said, gesturing to the closest zombie. "I mean, just look at those shoes. They're ruined."

A group of zombies is a pretty terrifying prospect at the best of times, but when they suddenly start lurching at high speed toward you, they're truly heart-stopping in their horrifying-ness. That was exactly what happened next, and it did Arty's nerves no favors whatsoever.

"Actually, change of plan," Sam shouted. "Run!"

They all turned sharply and set off away from the undead horde. Arty always took a while to build up speed, but he eventually gained a sort of terrible momentum, like a hippo on roller skates.

He lumbered through a garden, crashing straight through the front fence and out through the back. Sam, Emmie, and Phoebe hurried along behind him, with the pack of hungry undead hobbling along in hot pursuit.

Arty kept running until his legs and his lungs all got together and decided they'd had quite enough of that, thank you very much. He puffed and panted to a stop at the edge of the park.

Just beside them was the children's play area, complete with swings, a slide, a seesaw, and a colorful wooden playhouse with a rainbow painted on the roof.

"Let's hide in here," Arty wheezed. He pulled open the bright yellow door, then screamed as a shape came scrambling out of the shadows before he could step inside.

"It's not my fault! It's not my fault!" whimpered the figure, as he fell facedown onto the rubber flooring of the play area, then *boing*ed back up into a standing position.

"Professor Pamplemousse!" said Sam. "You're not going to believe what's happened."

"Everyone's started turning into zombies and they're trying to eat everyone else?" babbled the professor.

Sam nodded. "Okay, maybe you will believe it."

"It's not my fault," Pamplemousse whimpered. "I was only trying to mix a lotion for my sore knee." His eyes darted across the group. "It went a bit wrong," he said. (Pamplemousse was definitely a contender for the International Understatement of the Year award.) "Something quite terrible happened to Simon Stumble after I spilled it on him yesterday."

"Did it make his hair do that ginger electro-fizz thing?" Phoebe asked.

"His hair has always been like that," Emmie sighed. "He means it turned him into a zombie."

"How was I to know?" the professor sobbed, then spent the next few seconds making some high-pitched babbling sounds until Sam shook him by the shoulders.

"Pull yourself together, Prof," Sam commanded. "It can't be that bad."

"People are turning into zombies!"

"Right. Well, yes, that is pretty bad,

actually," Sam admitted. "But there must be something we can do!"

"Well . . ." Pamplemousse pondered, "there's the Town Hall. They've got plans there for all sorts of emergencies. Floods. Fire. Plagues of the living dead. We should go there."

"And then what?" Emmie asked. "We just hide?"

The professor began patting his coat pockets. "Actually, now that I think about it, there may be something we can do. Now, let me see, where did I put them—"

A low groan from nearby interrupted him. Everyone turned to see Mr. Gristle the local butcher walking their way. He gripped a cleaver in his meaty hand. His white apron wasn't actually white any longer. It was completely red! Well, it was mostly red, with two green smudges at the knees where he must've fallen on the grass. But ignore them. Just pretend it was all red, because that's scarier.

"Ah, Mr. Gristle, it's just you," said Professor Pamplemousse, letting out a sigh of relief. "I'm glad you're here. That cleaver of yours might come in handy. You see, there are a number of individuals roaming around who are extremely keen to munch on our—"

"Braaaaaiiins!" groaned the butcher.

"Precisely!" said the professor, nodding. As he did, he noticed the butcher's head bobbing up and down in time with his. "Um . . . why are you staring at me like that, Mr. Gristle?" he asked. "I haven't got something on my face, have I? Now, that *would* be embarrassing."

"Uh, P-professor," Arty whispered.

"Not now, lad. I'm talking with Mr. Gristle here."

"No, but—" Sam began, before a hiss from Mr. Gristle silenced him.

The butcher lunged, his wobbly, big face puckering up with hungry rage. Teeth the color of fine English mustard snapped shut just inches from Pamplemousse's face, which suddenly went very pale indeed. Pamplemousse blinked in surprise as Mr. Gristle raised his blood-soaked cleaver above his head and prepared to swing.

How to Spot a Zombie

Think someone you know might secretly be a zombie? Here are some clues to watch out for.

- Their face is hanging off.

- They're trying to eat you.

- They smell like a granny's armpit.

- They walk like someone's stolen their knees.

- They moan a lot (and not about the state of your bedroom—that's probably just your mom).

- Flies follow them everywhere and worms have parties in their hair.

- Their eyes are really creepy. (Emmie made me add this one.)

CHAPTER FIVE

For a teacher, Professor Pamplemousse could be dead thick sometimes. He never noticed when his students played pranks on him, and he definitely never noticed when the other teachers did, either. Rumor has it he once got lost in the staff room for three days, before eventually being led to safety by a janitor in a brightly colored vest.

And he appeared blissfully unaware that Mr. Gristle the butcher was all of a sudden only interested in one particular cut of meat. . . .

"Braaaaaiiins!" grumbled Mr. Gristle, and he swung with his cleaver.

"Look out!" cried Sam, shouldering Pamplemousse out of the way. The cleaver swished past Sam's face. He paused for a moment, expecting to see an ear or a slice of nose *schlopp* down onto the pavement, but as luck would have it,

neither one did.

Pamplemousse rounded on him, wagging a finger. "You could have really hurt me there," he scolded. "Whatever were you thinking?"

"Zombie!" Sam shouted.

Pamplemousse frowned. "What did you call me?"

"No, not you," said Emmie, pointing past the teacher to where Mr. Gristle was shuffling closer. "Him."

The teacher narrowed his eyes and studied the butcher's vacant expression and gnashing jaws. "Oh yes, you may well be right," he said.

And then he ran away, crying his eyes out, directly toward where the other zombies had been hanging about earlier, up to no good.

"No, not that way," Arty shouted, but he was already too late. Professor Pamplemousse had run off without looking back.

"What should we do?" asked Emmie.

"Die of fright?" suggested Arty.

"We need to come up with a plan," said Sam.

"Well, FYI, there's no way I'm running on the grass," said Phoebe. "Not in these shoes."

"Braaaaaiiins!" said Mr. Gristle.

Everyone else exchanged glances. "Oh yeah," said Sam, swallowing nervously. "I forgot about him."

The cleaver swished clumsily toward Sam, but he ducked out of its path. Arty caught him by the sleeve and dragged him out of the butcher's reach.

"Run!" Arty yelped, and he stumbled away with Emmie and Sam right on his heels.

"Like, *hello*?" sighed Phoebe. "Were you even listening? I can't run in these shoes."

"Then leave them!" snapped Emmie.

Phoebe's hand flew to her mouth. "Leave them? Are you crazy? Do you have any idea how much these cost?"

Mr. Gristle's pudgy hand slapped down onto Phoebe's shoulder with a sound like a salmon being hit by a spade. Phoebe went rigid. Her once-immaculate hair stood on end. "I'm leaving the shoes!" she decided. Then she kicked them off and raced barefoot across the park.

"This way," panted Arty, ducking under the jungle gym and through a gap in the trees. He stopped when he spotted several shapes shambling toward him, their teeth chewing the air like it was made of toffee. But not the licorice kind, because licorice-flavored toffee is revolting, and anyone who says otherwise is a filthy liar.

In an unusual twist of fate, Professor

Pamplemousse had once attempted to
make licorice-flavored toffee in his lab.
It didn't work, though, because—unlike
licorice-flavored toffee—it actually tasted
all right.

Anyway. Where were we? Oh yeah,
zombies and that.

"Not this way!" Arty corrected. "Definitely
not this way!"

They turned and wove past the swings and
around the merry-go-round. A path led off
to the right, up a steep hill known locally as
Devil's Peak, for reasons far too complicated
to go into right now.

A mad-haired old man with milky-white
eyes exploded from the trees. (By which
I mean he jumped out quickly. He didn't
literally explode or anything. That would have
been hideous.) His fingers found Arty's shirt.

His jaw dropped open and hunger blazed in those cold, dead eyes. A terrible, high-pitched, and piercing scream split the air. It took Arty a moment to realize the screaming was coming from him.

"Get it off! Get it off!" he gibbered.

Sam dodged left and right, his hands raised, preparing to push. The zombie's teeth chomped closer and closer to Arty's face.

"Hurry up!"

"But . . . it's an old man," Sam said at last. "I can't hit an old man."

Thwam! Emmie shoved the zombie hard in the chest, sending it sprawling back into the bushes. "There!" She scowled. "Now, come on, let's go this way."

She turned, but another group of zombies blocked the path.

"Or maybe not."

"I'm going to die," said Phoebe, glumly.
"I'm going to die in a park with no shoes on.
And I don't even want to *think* about how my
hair looks."

"No one's going to die," said Sam. A nearby
zombie tripped, fell, and impaled himself on a
jagged tree stump. "Okay . . . maybe that guy.
But not us. My house isn't far. We can hide
out inside."

There was a murmur of agreement from
Emmie and Arty. "Any questions?" asked
Sam.

Phoebe's hand shot up. "Sorry, I wasn't
listening," she said, lowering her arm. "What's
happening?"

"We're going to my house," said Sam.
"Now . . ."

Phoebe's hand shot up again. Sam did his
best to remain patient. "Yes?"

"No, I meant what's happening in general? We're not going to get eaten, are we?"

"Maybe," said Emmie.

"Oh, right. I see," said Phoebe. Then she began to scream.

"Shh! Shut up!" Sam whispered. He clamped a hand over Phoebe's mouth, trapping another scream before it could give them away. "Come on," he barked. "If we want to stay alive, we need to move now!"

It took longer than usual to get from the park to Sam's house. This, as you'll know if you've been following the story, was due to the large groups of the living dead roaming around the place, up to all sorts of flesh-eating mischief.

Sam's house was empty, which was a relief on one hand and quite worrying on the other. It was a relief because an empty house was by its very definition a house without any zombies in it. But it was also worrying because although Sam was staying at Arty's while his mom and dad were away for the weekend, he didn't know if they were up to their armpits in zombies, too, or if the outbreak was confined to Sitting Duck. He hoped his parents were having a nice time and not being eaten alive somewhere. It would be a real downer on their weekend if they were eaten.

As soon as Sam picked up the key from under the plant pot, he and the others were through the door and getting to work to make the place safe. Sam headed out into the garden to build a trip-wire system that would alert them if zombies got close to the house. Arty searched inside the house for things they could use as weapons. Emmie, meanwhile, tried to calm Phoebe down by slapping her across the face over and over again. Despite the situation, Emmie quickly started to enjoy herself and she was quite disappointed when Phoebe went and spoiled the game by snapping out of her daze.

Zombie Trip-Wire Alarm System

A trip-wire alarm system is a great way of alerting you to approaching zombies, door-to-door salesmen, or people in cardigans droning on about life after death. Here's how to set one up:

1. Choose the right spot. Near the ground usually helps.

2. Get a long piece of string (or thread), then thread (or string) it across the area you want to protect. Tent pegs are ideal for tying the string (or thread) to. Bananas are not.

3. Make sure the string is nice and tight. You should be able to play it like a very boring, one-stringed guitar.

4. Attach noisy things to the ends of the string. Noisy things might include pots, pans, bells, and fire engines. Things to avoid might be feathers, custard, cotton candy, and clouds. Then sit back and wait for your enemies to approach.

When Sam came back in from the garden, Arty was showing off the weapons, like that guy from James Bond who shows off the weapons. You know the one.

"I call this one the Multispeed Undead Threshing Device," he announced grandly, holding up one of the items he'd found for the others to see.

"That's funny," said Sam. "My mom usually calls it a whisk."

"Tell me that's not all you found," groaned Emmie.

Arty held up the next object. "I think you'll like this one. I've named it the Bristly Brain Basher."

"It's a toilet brush," sighed Emmie.

"Ew." Phoebe grimaced. "Toilets." Then she went back to rubbing her aching face.

As Emmie
and Arty
continued
to bicker, Sam
clicked on the
radio. There was a sudden
squawk of static
followed by a
familiar voice
floating over the airwaves. It was the
mayor.

"This is the mayor," he said. (See, told
you.) "It has come to my attention that
some things have been happening that,
all things considered, probably shouldn't
be happening. Not entirely sure what the
story is, but it's probably best if everyone
tootles along to the Town Hall until we
can figure out exactly what's happening

and to whom it's happening. See you there!"

The radio hissed off into silence.

"Right, then," said Emmie. "You heard the man—let's go."

"What, out there?" gasped Arty.

"Well, I doubt they'll bring the Town Hall here," Emmie said. "So yes, out there."

Arty sat down on Sam's sofa and almost hurt himself with the TV remote control. "No chance," he said. "We're safe here."

Emmie turned to Sam. "Tell him."

Sam shrugged. "I can see his point. We did nearly get eaten."

"You're not scared, are you?" Emmie scowled.

Sam shook his head. "No. But Arty is."

"Terrified," Arty agreed.

"So I can't leave him by himself," Sam said.

Emmie sighed. "Phoebe? Are you coming to the Town Hall?"

Phoebe snorted. "No way. It totally reeks of old people."

"Right. Fine." Emmie shrugged. "I'll go by myself, then. I don't mind."

"What?" spluttered Arty.

"You can't do that!" cried Sam. "What about the zombies?"

"What about them? We've seen, what? A dozen? It's hardly a plague, is it? It's barely even a social gathering." Emmie crossed her arms. "You lot stay here and wait for the zombies to come knocking if you like."

"I don't think zombies bother to knock," Arty pointed out.

"Well, whatever they do," Emmie said. "If you want to wait for them to do it, you go ahead. Me? I'll be safely tucked up in the Town Hall with everyone else."

"No way," snorted Arty. "You wouldn't dare just go off on your own!"

Sam sighed. That had done it.

"Wouldn't dare? *Wouldn't dare?*" Emmie snapped. "Just you watch me!"

And with that, before anyone could make a move to stop her, she yanked open the back door and was gone.

Converting Household Gadgets into Weapons

When caught up in a zombie apocalypse, the important thing is to not panic. Actually, that's not true. Definitely panic.

These things are going to try to eat your face off! Panic, for goodness' sake. What are you, a robot?

While panicking, it's a good idea to arm yourself. Being armed will allow you to fool yourself into thinking you might get through the whole thing alive, when you and I both know there's no chance of that happening, right? Right.

So, if you're looking for inspiration for homemade weaponry, look no further:

1. The Slice 'n' Dicer

Set your toaster to its highest setting, stick in some slices of bread, and take aim. Three to four minutes later, those zombies had better watch out, as some charcoal-like bread might just take their heads off! But probably won't.

2. Fantastically Forceful Football-to-Face

Let's assume for a minute that you're an incredibly skilled footballer. And let's also assume that you can kick a football with the approximate force of a small cannon. Working on these assumptions, why not use your incredible skills to combat the living dead by blattering the ball off their heads as they try to eat you alive? Remember to ask for the ball back afterward, or you'll really only get one shot.

3. Laser Blast Rifle

You know how DVD players use a laser to read the disc? I'm fairly sure there's a way

you can strip that down and use the laser
and lens as part of a futuristic blaster rifle
with which to incinerate the living dead. I
mean, I don't have blueprints or anything,
but I reckon it'd be straightforward enough.
Alternatively . . .

4. Rolling Pin

Sort of speaks for itself, really.

CHAPTER SIX

In the silence that followed, Sam wondered if he should have stopped Emmie from going. Arty wondered if the army would sweep in to save them from the zombie hordes.

Phoebe wondered how her hair was looking. She took her compact mirror from her ridiculously small bag and checked her reflection. Her hair looked like a bird's nest and the freshly applied lip gloss was already smudged.

"We shouldn't have let her go," Sam fretted. "Anything could happen to her."

"She could be eaten alive." Phoebe nodded.

"Yeah," said Sam.

"Or get mistaken for a zombie and have her brains bashed in."

"Yep," said Sam.

"Or be torn limb from limb by a pack of—"

"Yes, thank you, Phoebe. We get the idea," Sam said. He paced anxiously around the living room. "We shouldn't have let her go."

From out in the back garden there came a loud clatter of pots and pans. Something had snagged on Sam's trip wire. They all held their breath. Then Sam let out a sigh of relief when there came a *rat-a-tat-tat* on the kitchen door. *It must be Emmie!* Sam thought. After all, as Arty already mentioned, zombies don't knock on doors.

"Emmie, you came back!" he said, grinning broadly as he pulled the door wide open. The smile fell away immediately. The thing on the doorstep wasn't Emmie. Not unless Emmie had rapidly put on weight, become a fully grown man, and died.

"Braaaaaiiins!" groaned Mr. Gristle, and he stumbled forward into the house, hands grabbing for Sam as a dozen or more zombies pushed in behind him. YOU SEE! Zombies *do* knock on doors sometimes! Even Arty can't be right all the time.

Sam danced back as Phoebe and Arty rushed into the kitchen. He tried to push the door closed, but the zombies were already inside, their mournful moans filling the room and rattling the dishes in the sink.

"Change of plan," Sam announced. "We need to go. Now!"

The zombies seemed to be taking a special interest in Arty. Whether they could

sense his larger-than-average brain or liked the look of his plumper-than-average body, it was impossible to say, but they swarmed toward him like piranhas. But with arms and legs and that. And not in water. So not much like piranhas at all, really. I take that back.

"S-stay back," Arty warned, fumbling in the waistband of his pants. "I'm warning you, don't make me use *this*!"

"Hey, that's my toothbrush," Sam protested.

"It's a personal Bristly Eye Poker!" Arty replied. Then he squealed in terror as Mr. Gristle's sausagelike fingers wrapped around his neck.

"Braaaaaiiins!"

"Hey, butcher-man, *meat* my fist!" cried Sam, swinging a punch at Mr. Gristle's head.

It sent the zombie staggering backward, knocking over several other zombies like bowling pins.

"*Meat* my fist?" snorted Phoebe. "OMG, that was so lame."

"I thought it was quite clever, actually," wheezed Arty.

Sam flashed him a smile. "Thanks," he said. "Now come on, out the front door!"

They dashed back into the living room, clambered over the sofa, and raced for the door. Sam had stacked furniture in front of it to keep the zombies out. He and Arty set to work clearing it all away again as the living dead struggled to bypass the obstacle of the sofa. (Zombies can be surprisingly fast, but they aren't good climbers.)

"Hurry up!" Phoebe urged.

"You could help, you know!" Sam replied.

"*Hello?* Do you know how long it took to get these fingernails perfect? They might break."

"We might die!" Arty cried.

Phoebe crossed her arms. "Then at least I'll die with perfect fingernails."

With a roar of effort, Sam shoved a sideboard aside, just as the zombies prepared to lunge. "Done!" he cried. He pulled open the door.

And then he stopped dead, as he realized he was looking right down the double barrels of a particularly nasty-looking shotgun.

*

How a Zombie Virus Spreads

1. Zombie bites

2. Zombie sneezes

3. Zombie kisses (don't ask)

4. You know when a zombie explodes and a little bit gets in your mouth and you're all, like, "Eww, that was disgusting. I'm going to throw up"? That.

Let us journey back in time now, my friends. Back to a time before man had set foot upon the Earth, when dinosaurs roamed and the planet's crust was a shifting mass of inhospitable molten rock.

Then let us journey forward in time again. Forward to a time when Emmie had just left Sam's house, and the planet's crust was largely quite nice, depending on whom you asked.

Emmie wasn't happy. Given the morning's events, that wasn't entirely surprising, I suppose—but it wasn't the zombies who had made her unhappy. It was Sam and the others.

Don't get me wrong—even though she had enjoyed slapping Phoebe across the face, she was delighted to be away from her. She was quite annoyed at Sam and Arty, though, who seemed to be taking this whole legions-of-the-living-dead thing a bit too seriously, if you asked her.

It was only a few zombies, and she didn't quite see what the big deal was. The army was probably already gathered at the Town Hall, where the rest of Sitting Duck would all be sitting down to a nice cup of tea and some cake.

Zombies, she thought. *A-Lot-of-Fuss-About-Nothing-ies, more like.*

Still, she figured it might not be a bad idea to grab her baseball bat from her garden, just in case she came across any flesh-eaters on the way to the Town Hall and had to batter their heads in for them.

Great-Aunt Doris was peering down at her from an upstairs window when Emmie vaulted over the fence and into her garden. Emmie gave her a quick wave and picked up the bat from where she'd left it lying on the grass. Her schoolbag was there, too, right where she'd abandoned it yesterday. She opened it, tipped out the books, and swung the straps over her shoulders.

"Oi!" hissed Doris, opening the window just a crack. "You dead?"

"What?"

"I said, *you dead?*"

Emmie shook her head. "Not that I've noticed."

Doris tutted. "More's the pity." She scowled. Then she slammed the window and swished the curtains closed.

Emmie watched the window for a few seconds, shrugged, and made for the front gate. A savage roar erupted from one garden over, followed by the high-speed whine of an electric weed trimmer.

Mr. Stringer, one of Great-Aunt Doris's neighbors, was racing along his garden path, holding the trimmer out in front of him like a jousting lance. Emmie wasn't sure what Mr. Stringer did for a living, but she suspected it had something to do with numbers, filing cabinets, or the color gray. He just had that sort of look about him. Normally.

Today he looked rather different. The mud-brown tie he usually had neatly fastened around his neck was now knotted around his head. His normally crisply pressed shirt was creased and bloodstained, and he had completely forgotten to put his pants on.

A group of zombies was making its way up

the path toward him, but Mr. Stringer didn't appear the least bit afraid. He charged at them, the spinny bit of his electric trimmer spinning good and proper.

"HAVE SOME OF THIS!" he roared as he reached the zombies. With a loud *boing* sound—which would've been pretty funny in any other situation—the electric cable attached to the back of

the trimmer went tight, and,

somewhere at Mr. Stringer's house, the plug pulled free of the wall.

The spinny bit stopped spinning.

Mr. Stringer stopped running.

"Oh dear," he said. Then the zombies were on him, chewing and munching and making a mess of his shirt that no amount of stain remover would ever be able to get out.

Emmie knew it was too late to save Mr. Stringer. Maybe if she found a bucket she might've been able to save *some* of him, but he wouldn't have been in any state to thank her for it. She turned and ran for the park instead, planning to cut through it toward the Town Hall and hopefully avoid stumbling upon any more grisly scenes.

On only her third step into the park, she slipped on the slick grass and landed perilously close to a puddle of gunk.

Professor Pamplemousse lay on the grass beside her. Or parts of him did, at least. Other parts were scattered here and there across the play area, and part of a leg was dangling from a nearby tree. By the looks of him, running away earlier hadn't worked out too well. Maybe Mr. Gristle had caught up with him in the end, or maybe he'd failed to spot some other undead maniac until it was too late. Alas, we'll never know for sure. Whatever happened, though, he wasn't going to be recovering in a hurry.

Emmie was about to get up and run when she spotted something sticking out of Professor Pamplemousse's top pocket. It was one of his kidneys.

But there was something else there, too. She looked closer and saw a number of little glass test tubes, each one containing a gloopy liquid and sealed at the top with a rubber stopper.

Emmie reached down, plucked them out,

and stuffed them into her backpack. As she straightened up, she spotted Arty's brother, Jesse. He was wandering around by the skate park, just a few yards from the play area. He looked confused and still half soaked from the water bombing, but then "confused" was Jesse's standard facial arrangement.

"Hey, Jesse!" she hissed. "Psst! Over here."

Jesse turned and Emmie immediately realized her mistake. Jesse's eyes were lifeless and dull. When he fixed his gaze on her, Emmie felt a shiver run down her spine. She tried to duck behind the half-pipe, but it was too late. Jesse had seen her.

And he was closing in for the kill.

Backpack Supplies for the Zombie Apocalypse

Good:	Bad:
Weapons	Homework
First-aid kit	A valuable piece of art
More weapons	A baby panda
Food	Rotten meat
Radio	A high-pitched alarm that won't shut up
Even more weapons	Anything weighing more than you do
Clean pants	A zombie

CHAPTER SEVEN

Sam and the others raised their hands. "Don't shoot!" Sam cried.

"No choice, I'm afraid," barked a gruff voice from the other end of the gun. "Suggest you duck, though, and be jolly quick about it."

Sam dropped to his knees, pulling Arty and Phoebe down with him. There was a sound like the belching of a thunder god, and lead spat from both barrels of the gun. Across the room, a zombie was transformed into a brightly colored smear on the wallpaper.

As the shooter lowered his gun and

hurried to reload, Sam recognized his next-door neighbor. "Major Muldoon," he said, slapping himself on the forehead. "I should have known!"

"Bang on, old bean," said the major, his bushy white mustache standing to attention. "And speaking of bangs . . ."

He fired again at the zombies, and two more zombies became damp stains on Sam's living room carpet. Sam thought his mom would probably be furious. Assuming she hadn't already been eaten, of course, in which case a messy carpet was probably quite low on her list of priorities.

"That should hold the blighters back for a moment," said the major, grinning proudly. "Bit of a rum situation this, eh, young Sam? End of the world, some say."

"Who says?" asked Arty.

Major Muldoon shrugged. "Well . . . me, mostly. Tallyho!"

He swung with his gun and blasted another approaching zombie. "But by *Jove* they make terrific target practice, what! I haven't had this much fun in years! *Ptchow! Bang!* And so on and so forth!"

"Oh, terrific," muttered Phoebe. "He's a maniac."

"Any idea what caused it?" Sam asked the major.

"Not the foggiest," the major replied. "Don't know, don't care. Shooting the blighters is ruddy good sport, though!"

"I think . . . I think I might know," said Arty, before the roar of another shotgun blast interrupted him. "At least I'm trying to formulate a theory, but it's a bit hard with all the groaning of 'braaaaaiiins' going on, and

the major shooting the place up." He took a deep breath. "I think this must've been caused by the gunk in Professor Pamplemousse's lesson."

"The stuff that hit Simon? But I thought zombies were the ones that bust out of graveyards?" asked Sam.

Arty nodded. "Yes, but the two chemicals Pamplemousse used must have combined to have the same effect. It makes people brain-dead and then brings them back as one of those—"

Blam!

Major Muldoon let out a loud "Hurrah!" as another zombie became part of the brain-mush that now painted the room like lumpy pink paint. Made of brains.

"Nice and easy to blast 'em in small groups," he said. He jabbed a thumb back over his shoulder. "Not so easy out yonder, though."

"What do you mean?" asked Sam.

Major Muldoon cracked the barrels of the gun and slid in two new cartridges. "Over half the town's been infected," he said. "It's like World War I out there, only with zombies and whatnot. Can't move for the blighters!"

Sam looked past the major. A chorus of low moans drifted in from somewhere outside.

"We're vastly outnumbered," the major continued, "and it looks to me like the hungrier they get the more jolly well angry they become! They'll be chasing us down like lions hunting zebra on the African plains."

Phoebe's hand shot up. "Which are we, lions or zebras?"

"The zebras," replied the major.

Phoebe's face fell. "Oh no!" she gasped. "Stripes make me look fat."

"Emmie!" gasped Sam. "Emmie's out there on her own."

Arty's face went even paler than usual, which meant it was very nearly invisible. "With a much more sizable contingent of the undead than she thought!"

"She was heading for the Town Hall," Sam said. "We should go after her."

"Jolly good idea," said Major Muldoon. "It's an easy place to fortify, heavy doors, high windows. You'll be safe there."

Arty's eyes lit up. "Safe? Yes. Safe is good! I like safe! Let's go!"

"Not so fast," said Major Muldoon. "It's a war zone out there. You won't survive two minutes stomping about with those ruddy great feet of yours."

Arty looked down. "What's wrong with my feet?"

"What you need is some of this," said the major. He waggled the thumb and pinkie of his right hand, then touched his nose twice with the index finger.

The others watched him carefully.

"And one of these," Major Muldoon continued. He tickled the top of his head, then formed a crocodile shape with his fingers and snapped them together.

Arty leaned in close to Sam. "What's he doing?"

"Having a mental breakdown," Phoebe muttered.

"Hand signals!" the major explained. "So you don't have to go bellowing to one another."

"Aaah, right," said Sam. "I thought you were having some kind of seizure."

"You three make your advance on the Town Hall, quick smart," the major urged. "I'll hang back here and keep these blighters off your back, or my name isn't Major Mushroom!"

"Er . . . but that isn't your name," said Sam.

"Isn't it? Not to worry!" laughed the major. "Tallyho!" he cried, and Sam, Arty, and Phoebe ran off, with the blasts from the shotgun ringing loudly in their ears.

Stop! Danger Ahead   **Stop! Nerds Ahead**   **Be Alert for Giant Bunnies**

Major Muldoon's Stealth Hand Signals

We're all fine!   **No, I tell a lie. We're definitely going to die.**

CHAPTER EIGHT

Emmie's grip tightened around the baseball bat until her knuckles turned white. She had her back pressed against the side of the half-pipe and was doing her best to keep out of sight. Not that it really mattered, though, because Jesse was shambling straight for her.

Well, there was no way she was going to let him eat her alive. Not today. Probably not tomorrow, either, although she *might* be up for being eaten alive on Tuesday, because nothing interesting ever happened on Tuesdays and it would help to pass the time.

Jesse's flapping great feet shuffled through
the grass. Emmie held her breath. This was it.

She jumped.

She screamed.

She swung.

The baseball bat crunched into Jesse's
stomach. He dropped to his knees, clutching
his guts, and then toppled sideways onto the
grass.

"What did you do that for?" he gasped.

"Aren't you a zombie?" Emmie asked.

"No!"

Emmie stared at him, then gave him another sharp *thwack* with the bat, just in case.

"Ow! Cut it out!"

"Well, what were you giving it all that for, then?" Emmie demanded, letting her face relax into a zombielike state of doziness.

"That's just my face!" Jesse snapped. He was telling the truth. They say the most dangerous people in the world are those who appear to be idiots but are secretly super smart. Jesse was a little bit like that—he looked like an idiot but he was, in fact, an idiot.

"Oh, sorry," said Emmie, helping him up. "You could probably get some sort of surgery."

"For my stomach?" Jesse winced. "It'll be fine in a minute."

"Actually, I meant for your face," Emmie said. Jesse's eyes narrowed angrily. "Just, you know, so people don't mistake you for a zombie," Emmie explained. "I'm just thinking of you here."

Jesse shook his head. "What a day," he muttered. "Water balloons, baseball bats. What next?"

"Flesh-eating monsters, probably," Emmie said.

Jesse shrugged. "Nah, they don't seem to bother with me," he said. He puffed out his broad chest. "Probably too scared."

"Or they think you're one of them," Emmie snorted.

"Yeah, yeah. Shut it," Jesse sneered, even though—deep, deep down—he was secretly quite hurt. Did he really look like a zombie? He hoped not. The last one he'd seen hadn't even had a forehead.

He shrugged, because even more deep down he didn't really care what Emmie thought. "I'm going back home," he told her, then he about-faced and stomped off.

Emmie watched him until he was out of sight. Then she glanced across the park in the direction of the Town Hall. She could already hear the moans and groans of the living dead closing in from all directions. She was going to have to fight her way to safety. Unless . . .

She thought about Jesse, with his vacant expression and his shambling walk. She thought about what he'd said—that the zombies had left him alone.

With a splat, Emmie applied a layer of mud to her skin and messed up her clothes. She let out an experimental groan and shuffled a few unsteady paces forward.

A smile spread like warm jam across her face. "If you can't beat 'em," she said, "join 'em!"

How to Fool a Zombie

- Torn clothes

- Mud on face

- Hair like a bird's nest

- Walk like you've wet yourself

- Intestines hanging out (not recommended)

CHAPTER NINE

When Sam, Arty, and Phoebe reached the Town Hall, they were delighted to discover everything was fine. All the zombies had been taken care of and there were bunnies sliding down rainbows having a rare old time for themselves.

Actually, that's a total lie. I just said that because what they actually found was pretty worrying, and I wasn't sure if your nerves could handle any more.

You see, what they really found were zombies. Lots of zombies. More zombies than they had ever

118

seen, in fact, all lumbering about looking hungry and moaning about brains the way zombies do.

"Well, that's disappointing," whispered Arty. "I was hoping for some bunnies sliding down rainbows or something. What now?"

"There's a back door," Sam said. "Let's try that."

"Ew," said Phoebe, crinkling her nose in disgust. "What *is* that smell?"

Arty pointed toward the zombies. "All the dead people. Just a guess."

"Being dead is no excuse not to wear deodorant, you know," Phoebe announced. All around them, zombies turned slowly in their direction.

"Oh, well done," Arty hissed.

"Well *someone* had to tell them," Phoebe replied. She let out a little yelp of shock when Sam grabbed her by the arm and yanked her toward the back entrance of the Town Hall.

"Hand signals," Arty reminded her. "That was why we were using hand signals, so the zombies wouldn't hear us."

"Well, I didn't know the hand signal for 'Ew, these guys stink,' did I?"

Arty pinched his nose. Phoebe tutted. "Okay, yes, I suppose that one makes sense," she admitted.

The back door of the building was half-open. Sam popped his head through the gap, had a quick look around, then pressed on inside. When the others were safely in, he pushed the door closed and slid across a heavy iron bolt to lock it.

"That should keep them out," he said.

Arty shivered. "Unless they're already in."

A narrow passageway led away from the door. Shadows hung like dark, heavy curtains at the far end. It was only when Sam and the others got closer that they discovered they really were curtains, and very nice they were, too. Sam pulled them aside and was immediately confronted by the red-nosed face of Mayor Sozzle.

"*Wuargh!* More zombies," the mayor gasped. He threw himself to his knees in front of them. "Don't eat me! Please! I'm too rich and important to die!"

"We're not zombies," Sam pointed out.

"Aren't you?" said the mayor.

He stood up and let out a sigh of relief. A waft of brandy breath hit Sam in the face. "Well . . . good for you," he said before launching into a fresh wave of sobbing hysterics. "Not that it matters, because we're all doomed anyway. Doomed, I tell you!"

He careered off with his arms flailing dramatically, managing to knock over a radio, six plastic cups, and a young secretary who happened to be in the wrong place at the wrong time.

The Town Hall had been turned into an emergency command center, filled with people staring at computer screens, listening to radios, and nibbling on sandwiches. Sleeping bags were stacked up in the corner and several kettles were boiling away, because if there's one way to see out a crisis, it's with a nice cup of tea and a nap.

Several aides in serious suits followed the mayor around, trying to keep him calm but failing miserably.

"I'm sure it's not that bad, sir," said one.

"Help will be here at any moment," said another.

"We're all going to die!" sobbed the mayor. He threw open one of the windows and leaned out. "Air! I need air! I can't breathe in here!"

Before the mayor could be grabbed by the zombies roaming about outside (which is even more painful than it sounds), one of the aides caught him by the waistband of his trousers and pulled him back in. The aide sighed with relief as the mayor flounced away from the window, then quickly came to regret getting involved when a zombie dragged him out through the window and fastened its teeth to his head.

Sam rushed over and closed the window, blocking out the sound of chewing and chomping and the snapping of bone.

Mayor Sozzle didn't seem to notice any of this. He just stumbled around, muttering about Sitting Duck's emergency zombie protocol, which he was pretty sure he'd seen lying around somewhere quite recently, and if everyone would just *shut up and stop dying for five minutes* he could remember where he put it.

He was halfway through searching a desk drawer for the fifth time when someone decided to turn on the big TV that sat in the corner. Everyone cheered when the words "Sitting Duck" flashed up on screen, because everyone likes to see their hometown on the television, don't they?

The cheering stopped quite quickly,

though, as the rest of the report played out.

"... deadly zombie virus," said the news anchor, "which has left government officials no option but to declare the town a quarantine zone. Military forces are on their way, and until such time as the zombie infection is contained, anyone attempting to leave Sitting Duck will be shot on sight. ..."

"Why would they do that?" gasped Mayor Sozzle.

"... So the infection doesn't spread any further, obviously," said the news anchor, and with that, someone hit the TV's mute button. The only sound in the room was the mayor sobbing uncontrollably. It didn't exactly fill Sam with confidence.

"I don't think Mayor Sozzle's going to

be much help," Sam said, watching the mayor lie down on the carpet and start sucking his thumb. "So until the army gets here, we're going to have to look after ourselves."

Arty nodded in agreement. Even Phoebe didn't argue. Sam glanced around the crowded room. "Now," he said, "where's Emmie?"

At that precise moment, Emmie was milling around outside, her arms outstretched, her mouth hanging open, and her feet shuffling her closer and closer to the Town Hall. She was slap bang in the middle of a group of zombies. Bits kept dropping off the one next to her. He had lost both arms and was down to just the one leg, although for a dead guy he was really quite good at hopping.

Scabby faces leered from the crowd as rotting bodies brushed by. Her heart pounded, her skin crawled, and her nostrils spasmed as the stink of the zombies swirled up them like nobody's business.

But it was working! Her plan was working! The zombies weren't even glancing her way, and the entrance to the Town Hall was only a dozen or so yards ahead. It had been surprisingly easy to sneak up behind them and shuffle her way into their ranks. They hadn't batted a rotting eyelid as she'd joined in, lurching and staggering with the best of them. She didn't want to sound bigheaded or anything, but she was clearly a genius. The plan was brilliant. Nothing could possibly go wrong now.

And then, quite out of the blue, Emmie sneezed. It was one of those sneezes that creeps up on you like a snot-filled ninja and explodes out of your nose with no warning whatsoever. Unfortunately for Emmie, zombies don't sneeze. Aside from the fact that they don't catch colds (they are technically

dead after all, and you can't get sicker than that), a strong sneeze would probably blow their heads off.

The zombies beside her stopped shuffling. Those ahead turned to face her. A hundred sets of jaws began gnashing hungrily in her direction as the undead horde spotted the impostor in their midst. . . .

Sitting Duck Zombie Protocol

In the (sadly) all too likely event that zombies invade the town of Sitting Duck, this official protocol will help ensure the number of people being eaten alive is kept to an absolute minimum. Follow these steps to ensure the safety of all Sitting Duck residents.

1. Avoid the Town Hall! You might be thinking it seems like an easy place to fortify, but trust us: It'll never keep zombies out. Going here spells almost certain death. If you are reading this official protocol inside the Town Hall, then make no mistake about it, you're dead.

You might as well lie down now and wait for it.

2. Don't panic! Unless you're in the Town Hall. Because then you're doomed.

3. If there are zombies outside your location, do not open the window to get fresh air. I mean come on, that's just common sense.

4. Do not put your arm in a zombie's mouth because you think it'll make a fun photo to laugh at later. It might, but you won't be around to appreciate the joke.

5. Do not allow the town to be "cured" of zombies by a nuclear missile. That's good advice anytime.

CHAPTER TEN

Everyone in the Town Hall heard the scream, but most of them pretended that they hadn't, because people are like that sometimes. Especially when there's a chance they'll get their brains munched.

Sam, Arty, and Phoebe rushed to the window and looked out. At first they weren't sure what they were looking at—it seemed as if the zombies were turning on one another. Then they realized the zombie they were turning on wasn't a zombie at all.

"Emmie!" said Sam.

"She needs help!" said Arty.

"She needs a makeover," said Phoebe. "I mean, like, OMG. What happened to her?"

"Will you forget about that stuff for one minute?" Arty snapped. "She's going to die out there!"

The word echoed around inside Phoebe's mostly empty head. *Die. Die. Die.* She realized then that she didn't want Emmie to die. Emmie was the only girl she knew in Sitting Duck, and if Emmie got eaten, then Phoebe's social circle would decrease considerably.

That just would not do.

With a bansheelike screech, and in a move so characteristically out of character it was terrifying in itself, Phoebe threw open the window and held a hand out to Emmie. "Quick, in here!" she cried, wishing she had worn gloves because Emmie looked even dirtier up close.

Emmie reached out a hand. Her fingers brushed against Phoebe's. Then she saw one of the zombies lunge forward, teeth snapping.

"Like, ow!" Phoebe gasped, pulling her arm away. "That was harsh," she muttered. Then she spotted the back of her hand and her face went pale. A half-moon shaped set of teeth marks was imprinted on her skin. As she stared, a trickle of blood crept along her fingers and dripped onto the floor.

"You've been bitten," Arty gasped.

Phoebe glanced at him. "That's . . . Is that bad?"

"You'll turn into a zombie," Sam said, which wasn't exactly the most tactful way of breaking the news. A card would have been nicer. One with *Sorry. You've Joined the Legions of the Living Dead* written on it, and a picture of a cute zombie with a goofy face underneath.

Phoebe nodded slowly. "Right," she said. "A zombie."

Then she dropped her little handbag and

ran, screaming, back along the passageway
and off into the dark twisting corridors of the
Town Hall.

"Don't mean to be a pain," said Emmie
sharply, "but *I'm about to be eaten out
here!*"

Sam and Arty yelped in fright and grabbed
her. Emmie kicked and scrambled her way in
through the window, booting a few zombies
square in the face as she did.

As Emmie slid down onto the floor,
Sam hurriedly closed the window behind
her. For a long time, Emmie just lay on her
back, breathing heavily and staring up at
them.

"All right?" Sam asked, at last.

"Yeah, not bad, not bad," Emmie replied.
"How did you get here?"

"Walked. You?"

"Watched my neighbor get eaten, attacked Jesse with a baseball bat, pretended to be a zombie, and almost died."

"Oh," said Sam, fighting back a grin. "Our way was quicker."

"Is Jesse okay?" asked Arty, adding *Please say no, please say no, please say no*, silently in his head.

"As okay as he ever is." Emmie shrugged.

Arty tried to hide the disappointment on his face. It wasn't that he didn't like his brother; it was just that life would be so much easier if he got eaten. Also, it would mean that Arty would get his bedroom, and he'd always wanted that bedroom.

Emmie looked around. "Where did Phoebe go?"

"She ran off," Sam said. "She's been bitten. We should find her."

Emmie nodded. "I can't believe she did that. She risked her life to save me."

"And after you were so horrible to her, too. . . ." Arty said. Emmie shot him a glare and he decided it was in his best interest to stop talking.

"Let's go," said Sam, but the mayor was suddenly blocking their path, his eyes as red as his nose. He wiped them on his sleeve, then pointed over to the TV just as someone turned the volume up.

Silence fell across the room. Everyone stared in horror at the news report.

News reports aren't very cheerful at the best of times. Unless you catch the bits at the end when they talk about skateboarding cats or babies who've learned to burp the alphabet or something. Normally, though, the news is pretty depressing viewing.

This news report was the worst of the lot. It went something like this:

The news anchor said there was a zombie plague sweeping through the town of Sitting Duck.

Everyone cheered when they heard their town's name on the television.

The presenter said the military had decided to take some decisive action.

A map of Sitting Duck appeared on screen.

Everyone cheered.

An artist's impression of a thermonuclear explosion wiping out the town of Sitting Duck appeared.

Everyone sort of mumbled a bit and looked uneasy.

The presenter explained that if they couldn't find a way to stop the zombies in the

next twenty-four hours,
the army would
have no choice
but to blow the
town of Sitting
Duck off the
map with
a massive
bomb,

FIG. 1.
SITTING DUCK

to avoid the devastating zombie infection
spreading.

The television was clicked off. Sam and the
others exchanged a worried look. The mayor
ducked under a desk.

"Twenty-four hours," said Sam. He looked
around the Town Hall. "This lot aren't going
to do anything, are they? It's up to us. We
need to find a way to fix this—after all, if
we could find the town's zombie protocol,

I'm pretty sure it'd specifically say to *avoid* nuclear explosions!"

Emmie blinked. There was something she'd forgotten. Something important.

"I've got it!" cried Arty. "I know how we can stop them!"

"How?" asked Sam, excited.

"Hypnosis."

Sam's excitement faded quite a lot. "Hypnosis?"

"We can hypnotize them into forgetting they're zombies!"

Emmie scratched her head. There was something she'd forgotten. There was definitely something . . .

"I'm not sure that'll work," said Sam.

"Of course it will!" yelped Arty, bouncing from foot to foot.

"Do you know how to hypnotize someone?" Sam asked.

Arty stopped bouncing. "I hadn't thought of that."

It was right then that Emmie remembered the thing she'd been trying to remember for the past minute or so. It was her turn to start hopping from foot to foot.

"Oooh!" she said. "Oooh, wait, I think I found something that'll help us!"

"*Hypnosis for Beginners*?" asked Arty.

"No, it's this. . . ." Emmie thrust a hand into her backpack and pulled out the little

liquid-filled test tubes she had found in Professor Pamplemousse's pocket. She handed them to Arty and he held them up to the light. "I got them off Professor Pamplemousse."

"Really? Did you see him?" Sam asked.

Emmie nodded. "Bits of him, yeah."

"This could be important," Arty gasped. "Professor Pamplemousse was trying to tell us something before Mr. Gristle came along. This must be it. It could be a cure!"

"So we could fix Phoebe?" Emmie asked.

Sam and Arty looked at her strangely. "If it works, it'll fix everyone," Arty said.

"Why so worried about Phoebe all of a sudden?" Sam asked. "I thought you didn't like her?"

"I don't," Emmie said with a shrug. "But she *did* try to save me, and now she might be a zombie. Which might be an improvement, actually. But if she's stuck as a zombie, she'll only hold it over me—you know what she's like."

"Even if it is a cure, how do we get them to swallow it?" Arty wondered. "We don't have a way of injecting them, so we need them to ingest it in some way."

Emmie reached down and picked up Phoebe's bag. Rummaging inside, she found a pink lip gloss that was all glossy and glittery, and smelled faintly of strawberries. "What if we put some of the cure in this?" she suggested. "Flesh-eating monster or not, I bet Phoebe won't be able to resist slapping some of this on if she sees it."

"Good plan," said Sam. Outside, the streets were darkening as night crept sneakily overhead. "But we should get some rest now and look for her in the morning. If we're going to save Sitting Duck from being blown to bits, we're going to need to get some rest."

Emmie's brain wanted to disagree with this idea, but her body had already been completely sold on it and was slumping down onto a chair even as her brain was trying to come up with a sensible argument. It had been a long, exhausting day, but even as she rested her head on the arm of the chair, she knew the sounds of the zombies outside meant there was no way she'd manage to fall asleep.

Emmie fell asleep.

A moment later, Arty fell asleep, too, and with the clawing fingers of the living dead scraping against the windows, Sam settled down for the long, lonely wait until morning.

The Stages of a Zombie Transformation

1. "Hey, that crazy guy just bit me!"

2. Headaches and dizziness

3. "I don't feel too good."

4. Death

5. Back again

6. "Braaaaaiiins!"

7. Shuffling about a bit

8. "BRAAAAAIIINS!"

9. Running very fast and biting people

10. Shot by Major Muldoon

CHAPTER ELEVEN

The search for Phoebe began early the next morning and took them all through the Town Hall. They searched in rooms filled with terrified-looking officials all shouting at one another. They checked in storage closets stacked high with chairs, tables, and terrified-looking officials all shouting at one another. They even checked down in the basement, where a single terrified-looking official was wandering around in circles, shouting at himself.

It was only when Emmie took a break from searching to use the bathroom that she finally tracked Phoebe down. She was standing in front of the big bathroom mirror, staring blankly at her own reflection.

This was not entirely unusual for Phoebe. She was always staring at her own reflection, although her skin didn't normally look so withered and gray. The blood oozing from her eyes was new, too, and based on the available evidence, Emmie deduced that Phoebe was quite probably now a zombie.

This theory was confirmed a moment later, when Phoebe spun on the spot and lunged, her mouth wide open and her perfectly polished teeth bared. She barreled into Emmie and they both stumbled out into the corridor in a tangle of arms and legs. They landed right by where Arty and Sam had been waiting.

As soon as they hit the floor, Phoebe's head

snapped up. Her eyes locked on to Arty's skull and her tongue flicked hungrily across her blue lips. She pounced off Emmie and onto Arty instead, slamming him against the wall and getting right up in his face, all hissing and snarling and everything.

"Get her off! Get her off!" yelped Arty. He wedged his forearm across Phoebe's throat in a desperate attempt to keep his brains where they were supposed to be.

Emmie fumbled in her pockets for the antidote-flavored

lip gloss. "One sec," she said. "Just keep her busy."

"How?" sobbed Arty.

"I don't know! Let her nibble an ear off or something!"

Arty's eyes almost bulged out of their sockets. "What?!"

"We can cure you afterward," Emmie said.

"It won't grow my ear back!"

Phoebe twisted free from Arty's grip and lunged at him with snapping teeth. Sam drove his shoulder into her stomach, knocking her back. She spat and snarled, and made to attack again.

"I'm sure it's in one of these pockets," Emmie muttered, but Sam and Arty were no longer listening. They threw themselves at Phoebe, using their combined body weight (which, thanks mainly to Arty, was quite a lot) to shove her back through the bathroom door.

Sam grabbed a cleaning cart and wedged the door closed. He and Arty took a moment to get their breath back as Phoebe groaned and growled and hurled herself against the other side.

"I've never seen her that worked up before," Arty wheezed.

"I have," said Sam. He shuddered. "That sale at the shoe shop last month."

"Found it!" announced Emmie, looking up. "Where's she gone?"

Sam and Arty pointed at the door. Emmie glowered at them.

"What did you do that for? I could have cured her."

"She almost ate us!" Arty panted.

Emmie shook her head. "You've got to make such a drama out of everything," she sighed. "We need to go in there and fix her up."

"I vote we leave her as she is," Arty said. He raised a hand. "Who's with me?"

Sam raised his hand, too. "Even with the whole trying-to-eat-our-faces-off thing, she's actually slightly less annoying than normal."

Phoebe had fallen silent, as if listening to what was being said about her. Emmie shook her head in disgust at the boys, then pulled the cart out of the way.

"I'm changing her back," she said. "For better or worse."

She held the lip gloss up in front of her like a very small sword, pulled open the bathroom door, and stepped inside.

She stopped when she saw that the

bathroom was empty. Cold wind swirled in through a broken window.

Phoebe was gone.

Emmie slumped back out of the bathroom. "It's no use," she said. "She's run off. We'll never be able to cure her now."

"We will," Sam promised. "We'll cure her and everyone else. Otherwise Sitting

Duck is going to be blasted off the face of the Earth."

"But what can we do?" fretted Arty. "There's no way we can spread the cure quickly enough."

"Unless . . ." said Sam. He thought for a moment, pausing to stroke his beard. Except he didn't have one. So it was just his chin, really. "I think I've got a plan," he announced. "What if we lured the zombies all together in one place?"

Arty frowned. "Lured them with what?"

"You," said Sam.

"What? Why me?"

"You saw how Phoebe reacted," Sam said. "Zombies are drawn to you. It's like they can smell your massive brain or something."

"Oh, so because I'm the most intelligent I get to be zombie bait?" Arty said. "In what way is that fair? And how would having them all together in one place help us anyway? We've still got no way of administering the cure."

Sam grinned. "Yes, we do," he said. He reached into his backpack and pulled out a handful of unfilled balloons. (See, I told you they'd be worth remembering.) "We fill these with water and add a few drops of the cure to each one."

"Then we splatter the zombies right in their ugly faces!" Emmie cried. "Brilliant!"

Arty stroked the nonexistent beard he had on his face, too. "That . . . that just might work." He took a deep, steadying breath. "O-okay," he stammered. "Count me in!"

Zombie Invasion Stat Round-Up

Innocent people eaten: 348

Zombie heads mashed in: 175

People infected with virus: 2,327

Limbs fallen off: 82

People who accidentally died after slipping on banana skins while fleeing from a pack of pursuing zombies: 1

Number of times the word "Braaaaaiiins" was said: $6{,}427^{1/2}$

CHAPTER TWELVE

Getting the zombies to follow them turned out to be fairly easy. Sam, Arty, and Emmie snuck out of the Town Hall. They shouted, quite loudly, "Oi, zombies!" Then they pointed at Arty's head a bit, and all the undead came running.

And that was part of the problem. The undead came *running*. They didn't shuffle or shamble like a gang of sleepwalkers out for a stroll. They ran. Properly ran. Very, very fast.

"Starting to regret this now!" panted Arty, as he clattered along behind the much speedier Sam and Emmie. His great flapping feet slapped the concrete as he sprinted for his life, but it wasn't enough to drown out the gnashing and snarling of the hundred or so zombies who were racing up behind them.

They ran up the main street and ducked beneath Bendy Bridge. Still the zombies followed, tumbling and clambering over one another, their terrible jaws drawing closer with every toothy snap.

"Can't . . . keep . . . running," Arty wheezed. Emmie and Sam grabbed an arm each and dragged him along between them.

"Almost there," Sam said. "Just a little bit farther!"

They twisted down another street and saw Jesse wandering around looking stupid. Emmie's eyes widened in surprise. "He's *still* okay! Unbelievable."

Jesse's head snapped up. "Braaaaaiiins," he hissed. Then he lunged for them.

"Oh no, my mistake," Emmie said with a gulp.

Finding some hidden reserve of strength, Arty charged, head lowered like a battering ram. He thudded into Jesse, sending him tumbling to the ground.

"That's for the liquid soap in the cola!"

Arty hollered. "You're just lucky I couldn't find a shark!"

And then he, Sam, and Emmie were off running again, Jesse and the other zombies snapping at their heels.

"We're not going to make it," Emmie gasped. "We're not going to make it!"

They turned a corner and the school loomed right ahead of them.

"We're going to make it!" Emmie cheered, and the sight of the school gave them an extra burst of speed. They thundered through the gates and up the steps.

"The doors are open!" Sam cried, barely able to believe their luck.

"Presumably when the infection broke out yesterday, the teachers forgot about matters of building security," Arty replied.

"Discuss later," Emmie snapped, shoving them inside. "Hide now!"

They slammed the doors closed, just as the tide of living dead hurled itself against them.

"Quick, the bolts, the bolts," Arty yelped. "Lock the doors!"

With a satisfyingly heavy-sounding *clunk*, Sam slid the metal bolts into place. The doors shook and the hinges groaned, but they held fast. They rested their heads against the door frame, taking a moment to get their breath back.

"Well, that was close," Emmie panted.

"They *really* want to eat your brains," said Sam, flashing Arty a grin.

"Braaaaaiiins."

In the half-darkness of the entrance hall, the three friends froze. After a moment, Emmie quietly cleared her throat.

"Arty," she said. "Was that you?"

Arty shook his head. A bead of sweat trickled down his nose and dripped onto the floor. "No, you?"

"Nope," whispered Emmie. "Sam?"

"Wasn't me," Sam replied.

They turned around slowly. There, in the middle of the hallway, stood Phoebe. She shuffled forward, and as she did her vacant expression twisted into one of rage. Her eyes locked on Arty's skull and her pace picked up. Her arms reached out. She growled and hissed like a savage animal in an expensive dress.

She lunged at Arty, but Emmie blocked her path. When she held up the lip gloss, the effect on Phoebe was instantaneous. She stopped grasping and snarling and being all about eating brains. Instead, she became all about sparkly pink lip gloss.

She smacked her cracked lips together. They made a sound like dry leaves rubbing against an old lady's stubble. Her lifeless eyes fixed on the tube and she took a cautious step closer.

"It's working," Sam whispered. "She's going for it."

"Come on, Phoebe," Emmie urged. "You want this, don't you? It's all girly and pink, just the way you like it."

Phoebe's face was slack, her mouth hanging wide like the top of a fisherman's rubber boot. The rage that had gripped her was ebbing away as the lure of the lip gloss pulled her in.

Then, without warning, she let out a
sudden snarl. She snatched the lip gloss
and tossed the whole thing into her mouth.
Her teeth clamped down. The plastic tube
shattered and filled her mouth with an
explosion of glittery pink nonsense.

She lunged, all teeth and fingers and the
faint whiff of strawberries. Her eyes bulged,
her hands found Arty's hair, and her jaws
came down, down, down toward his terrified
wobbly face.

"Noooo . . ." Arty began to scream.

Phoebe stopped.

". . . ooooooo . . ."

Phoebe sniffed. Her tongue licked around
the inside of her mouth.

". . . ooooooo . . ."

"It's working," Emmie cheered.

". . . ooooh. So it is," said Arty, just as

Phoebe released her grip. Her face was already looking slightly more healthy. There was a tint of red to her cheeks, although that could easily have been from someone she'd eaten that morning. Her eyes were a little less lifeless, and she was making no attempt to eat anyone's brains. These, Sam reckoned, were all good signs.

"Now we need to take care of the rest," Sam said. "Arty, watch Phoebe. Emmie, come with me."

Sam and Emmie raced to the water fountains and began filling the balloons. A sudden banging on the window beside them made them jump. The mayor was pressed up against the glass, his face rotten and bloodied. Dozens more zombies pushed in behind him.

Krik.

A small crack appeared on the window. Hurriedly, Emmie finished dripping antidote into each projectile, trying to ignore the groaning and banging that suddenly seemed to echo from every corner of the school at once.

Carefully putting the filled balloons into the backpack, they scurried back to the main entrance, where Phoebe's appearance continued to improve. Arty caught the panicked look on his best friend's face.

"How bad is it?" he asked.

Sam breathed out. "Pretty bad," he admitted. "But we're going to fix it."

They made for the stairs, dragging Phoebe along with them. Their footsteps echoed through the empty school, all the way up the steps and over to the big double window on the second floor.

The area outside heaved with the undead. They stood several rows deep, shoving and pushing one another as they fought to get inside. Sam set his bag on the floor, the water balloons wibbling gently inside.

"Ready?" he asked. The others nodded. "It's zombie curing time."

CHAPTER THIRTEEN

The water balloons fell in much the same way as the ones in chapter three did. The first one landed with a massive great *sploosh* on the head of a particularly nasty-looking zombie in overalls.

A hiss of steam rose up from the zombie's head. The water had splashed those on either side of him, too, and now steam rose off them like it was going out of fashion.

Sam, Emmie, and Arty let fly with more of the balloons. They wibbled and wobbled and burst spectacularly, and as each one rained down, more and more steam rose up.

A hand clamped down on Arty's shoulder and he let out a high-pitched scream. He turned to find Phoebe squinting at him.

"Like, why does my mouth taste like raw meat?" she asked. She looked down at her clothes and let out a little yelp of horror. "I've got brains on my dress! That'll never come out."

Down below, the zombies who had already been hit by water balloons had stopped trying to get inside. They were rocking gently from left to right, their hate-filled expressions now more confused than anything else.

"Grab a balloon and get chucking!" Emmie barked.

To her amazement, Phoebe did as she was told. She picked up one of the balloons, hefted it in her hands for a moment, then threw it.

It went splat
down on
the zombies
directly below
them.

Sam, Arty, and Emmie continued the bombardment, and with a hiss the sound of hammering on the front door began to fade.

By the time Sam had hurled the final one, the crowd below was well and truly drenched. Most of them looked more than a little bewildered to find themselves dripping wet in the school yard. Those who had arms or legs hanging off looked

somewhat concerned. They limped away in the direction of the hospital, muttering unhappily under their breath.

Downstairs, Sam threw open the front doors of the school and they all stepped out into the sunlight. Mayor Sozzle was wandering around, scratching his head and loudly announcing that everything was under control. "Of course, this was all part of the plan," he proclaimed. "Everything went exactly as I always knew it would. No, please, no need to thank me."

"You can say that again," Emmie snorted. "It's us they need to be thanking."

Mayor Sozzle peered at the children in turn, then leaned in close. "Really?" he mumbled. "You sorted all this business out?"

Sam nodded. "The three of us."

"Four of us," Phoebe protested.

Mayor Sozzle nodded. "Right. Well . . . good. Thanks for that," he said, grinning. He straightened up and rubbed his hands together. "Now, time for a celebration, I think."

"Shouldn't you notify the authorities that everything is under control?" Arty asked.

Mayor Sozzle laughed. "Nah! Why should we tell those fuddy-duddies anything?"

"So they don't blow us up in a thermonuclear explosion," said Sam.

The smile fell from the mayor's face. He blinked. "Oh. Yes. Forgot about that," he said. Then he turned and ran all the way back to the Town Hall as fast as his wobbly legs would carry him.

The town of Sitting Duck was still in a right old state when Sam's parents returned. They picked their way through the rubble, completely failing to notice all the blood and body parts that were still waiting to be cleaned up.

Luckily, Sam had managed to swirl some disinfectant around the living room and rubbed away the worst of the stains before his mom spotted them. Major Muldoon had even arranged for a repairman to come and fix the holes he'd blasted in the walls with his gun.

"Put the kettle on, sweetheart," said Sam's mom, as she slumped down onto the sofa.

"What a trip," his dad said.

"I need a vacation just to get over the vacation!" laughed Sam's mom.

"Yes," agreed his dad. "And then we'd need a vacation to get over the vacation we needed to get over the vacation!"

"No, dear," said Sam's mom, very seriously. "That would be ridiculous."

"Sorry," mumbled Sam's dad. He looked up at his son. "Anything happen when we were gone?"

"This and that," said Sam with a shrug. "Nothing I couldn't handle."

"Good boy." His dad smiled.

"Now . . . about that tea," urged his mom. Sam leaned down and gave them a hug.

"Welcome home," he said, then headed to the kitchen to put the kettle on.

Sam whistled happily as he ran the cold tap. Had he looked out the kitchen window at just that moment, he would've seen the local butcher, Mr. Gristle, out for a walk.

Cleaver in hand.

Jaws chomping hungrily at thin air . . .

So You Were a Zombie

So you've suddenly found yourself standing in the street holding someone's half-chewed elbow and wondering how you got there. Don't worry, the answer's probably not as bad as you think—chances are you've simply been a flesh-eating zombie for a few hours.

Oh no, wait, that is pretty bad, isn't it?

But have no fear! You're not alone. Many of your friends, neighbors, and loved ones will have gone through exactly the same thing as you have. That's probably why you don't have any fingers on your left hand anymore, and why you have that bite mark on your forehead.

The trick is not to worry about it. Oh sure, you may have eaten old Maude from next door and you haven't seen your beloved pet hamster since you changed back, but that's all in the past. Put it behind you and move on. Just be sure to really clean your teeth before you do.

Read them all!

Disaster strikes the town of Sitting Duck again . . . and again . . . and again . . .

Available now!   Coming soon!

Read on for a sneaky look at the disaster-defeating wisdom we have coming up for you in the next book....

Disaster Diaries: Aliens!

Sam, Arty, and Emmie have barely gotten over a recent zombie infestation when their sleepy little town finds itself the victim of an alien invasion!

But the aliens are very small and kind of, well, cute—how dangerous can they be?

SPOILER ALERT: They're VERY dangerous. And when they disintegrate the mayor with their ray guns, it'll be up to Sam, Arty, and Emmie to save the day. Again.

Defend Yourself From an Alien Sneak Attack

So aliens have invaded your planet? Bummer. Don't worry, I've put together this list of techniques you might want to put into use should one of those pesky invaders try to kill you in unpleasant ways. Be aware that some of these techniques will only be effective against specific alien races. While it is possible, for example, to tickle a member of the Fluffpuffle race into submission, this strategy will be somewhat less effective against the captain of a Venusian Death Fleet.

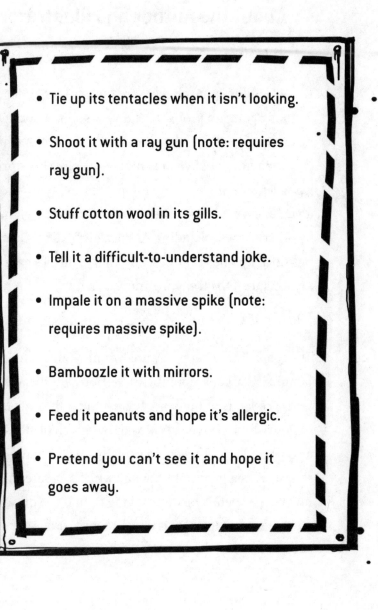

- Tie up its tentacles when it isn't looking.

- Shoot it with a ray gun (note: requires ray gun).

- Stuff cotton wool in its gills.

- Tell it a difficult-to-understand joke.

- Impale it on a massive spike (note: requires massive spike).

- Bamboozle it with mirrors.

- Feed it peanuts and hope it's allergic.

- Pretend you can't see it and hope it goes away.

About the Author and Illustrator

R. McGeddon is absolutely sure the world is almost certainly going to probably end very soon. A strange, reclusive fellow—so reclusive, in fact, that no one has ever seen him, not even his mom—he plots his stories using letters cut from old newspapers and types them up on an encrypted typewriter. It's also believed that he goes by other names, including A. Pocalype and N. Dov Days, but since no one's ever met him in real life, it's hard to say for sure. One thing we know is that when the zombie apocalypse comes, he'll be ready!

The suspiciously happy, award-winning illustrator **Jamie Littler** hails from the mysterious, mystical southern lands of England. It is said that the only form of nourishment he needs is to draw, which he does on a constant basis. This could explain why his hair grows so fast. When he is not drawing, which is a rare thing indeed, he spends his time trying to find the drawing pen he has just lost. He is down to his last one.

Create a Disaster Survival Kit

What would you put in your own
Disaster Survival Kit?

Maybe, like Arty, a Bristly Brain Basher
(aka toilet brush) is all you need to keep
enemies at bay?

Can you invent a more sophisticated
form of weaponry using a toilet roll or
an empty cookie tin?

Or do you really just want some sweets
and a clean T-shirt?

Pack your bag for the apocalypse and
keep it by the door in case of disaster!